Mrs. Bennet's Admonishments

Pride and Prejudice and Perseverance

by

DORI SALERNO

Always for Joyce

Dear Reader,

I hope you will not take offense at these gentle admonishments offered here. As a mother of five daughters, all well situated, and myself with many years of marriage completed, I offer these gentle admonishments as a guide. The journey through life for any well-bred woman is at times arduous. It is my wish that you find some comfort and guidance amongst these pages and avoid the errors I have made.

In all sincerity and good wishes,

Miriam Bennet

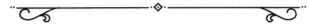

Suitors

"You don't need scores of suitors. You need only one... if he's the right one"... Louisa May Alcott

A young girl should take care not to pursue a gentleman or flaunt an abundance of suitors, lest she engender gossip that could sully her reputation. I am not saying to discourage the attention of suitors, for it is most pleasurable for young ladies to receive the attentions of gentlemen. Just be discreet.

On the problem of having no suitors —— do not despair! Keep in mind, the distraction of a suitor can severely interfere with one's own development. I know of many a pretty, young thing, so involved in maintaining a suitor's attention, that she neglects to put any effort into developing her own gifts, talents, and character. The end result is she becomes just a pretty appendage to a gentleman, who will quickly be

bored with her and will seek to replace her with another more accomplished partner.

Find your gift, your talent, your passion, something that will always sustain you, whether you be joined to another or not. As you practice and develop your skill: be it art, the pursuit of learning, good works, the love of travel, music, the sciences ———whatever path is open to you ——— follow it! And on your journey, you may find a suitor with like-minded sensibilities.

For the unrequited, those yearning for the affection of an indifferent suitor, I pray you keep your own counsel. If he is indifferent and you somehow manage through the sheer strength of your persistent affection to win him, believe me, ladies, you have won no prize. Your future together will always be out of balance with your seeking his embrace, catering to his every whim, grateful for any crumbs of affection he parsimoniously bestows. And he will feel put upon and resentful of your passion.

Merely switch the players and you will see that I am right. When a suitor you do not desire pursues you, do you not find ways to avoid him, and then moan and sigh about how odious you find his attentions?

That is not to say the balance of things can't shift. Many a young lady has re-evaluated a suitor she rejected, but usually only after his attentions appeared to be focused elsewhere. So, it is quite possible for a gentleman to miss the adoration of his ardent female admirer and esteem her more only if she appears preoccupied with the attentions of another.

Suitors must be suitable. If you enjoy parties and balls and he cannot withstand crowds or social gatherings, you may not be a match. Do not be blinded by handsome looks or financial position. Judge him by his behavior, not his words. Many a suitor can charm with pretty words and false promises. This puts me in the mind of Wickham with his charming ways and Darcy with his initial

odious, prideful, posturing.

Remember my Elizabeth—— though most likely secretly enamored of Mr. Darcy——did reject his first offer, which was filled with pride and condescension. Only after he was humbled and wooed her properly, did she accept him; thus, restoring an equal balance to their union. It is my belief, that the husband should be slightly more enamored of his wife, than she of him. Do not concern yourself if this is the case, for your esteem and love will far surpass his in the years of your marriage. My poor Lydia, so taken advantage of by that rogue, Wickham. At his death bed, he finally acknowledged the purity of her love and his unworthiness.

Seek balance. Keep your counsel about your affection until you are sure of its return and that he is worthy of your esteem. He must declare first. Even when it is time to profess the vows——hold fast! Be adamant. Though it is not the tradition, insist to the vicar that the groom make his vow

first with yours to follow. I have witnessed many a bride left standing under the briar, her commitment fresh upon her lips only to hear the groom recant.

Weddings

"In everything the purpose must weigh in with the folly"….. Shakespeare

The most important point to remember is it is just a day, you the blushing bride, he the stalwart groom——but through the folderol of it all——hold on to the reality that it is the marriage which is the most important thing ——not the wedding! Some of you may remember my experience with weddings: one, a glorious event, the double

wedding of Jane and Lizzy, and one, almost a non-event, the supposed Gretna Green of Lydia.

Whatever the circumstances, if you are the bride——Yes, with your choice of gown, attendants, locale and festivities it will be "your day", just remember to include the groom in the planning. And consider the reality of finances. So often one hears of couples having almost Bacchanal events set in exotic locations, with unlimited wine, food and merriment——later realizing what was spent on one day of celebration could have made a generous payment on a country or city abode. Traditionally the responsibility of wedding costs falls upon the bride's family. Talk with your family. Make sure they are not carrying an undue burden by putting home or savings at risk.

If you are the mother of the bride, remember it is her prerogative to choose her gown. No matter if she chooses something not to your taste or you feel it is unflattering to her, I urge you to bite your

tongue or at least choose your words carefully.

To this day, I regret as a young bride-to-be, being swayed by the opinion of others. While my gown design was flattering both in style and color with the cream tones complimenting my coloring, the bonnet proposed was less than complimentary. The design of the derby sported a short veil in the front, to be flipped to the back upon presentation to my husband. The veil then folded into a long flowing train of tulle attached to the back of the bonnet. It put me in mind of riding horses, and as I was no horsewoman, seemed absurd.

My heart had been set upon wearing a small circlet of garden flowers. My only chance of "acting the fairy princess" had just evaporated. The argument for the derby design was that it was needed to offset the simplicity of the dress. The fashion doyennes prevailed, and I walked down the aisle with the ridiculous hat rakishly perched upon my head. Once the ceremony was completed, I tossed it in the air, never to see where

it landed.

My girls were more fortunate in their gown choice. Mrs. Robbs, our local seamstress, had known them all their lives, and made their gowns reflect their individual tastes. Jane's was a frothy affair with tiers of lace, and Lizzy's, a study of understated elegance with a high lace collar, mutton sleeves and tight lace from elbow to wrist.

Collaborate on the choice of food and festivities and do help with the invitations. Consult as needed, but unless the Bride's wishes are totally unreasonable, try to give sway to her requests. I did prevail upon the girls to combine their wedding celebrations. We are a small county, and three celebrations in a row would have been most taxing. I had just completed a post-wedding reception for Lydia a few months before, and I felt it was too much to ask for attendance to two more weddings and receptions.

Be aware that some fathers of the bride see it as their duty to "hold the line" on finances. Mr.

Bennet remained like- minded for Lizzy and Jane's wedding celebration, wanting Darcy and Bingley to host the event. So improper and miserly of him! I almost boxed his ears! But I smiled, soothed and coaxed and was able to bring him 'round'. The mother of the bride is the arbiter of her husband's financial outlay, be it excessive or miserly, and her daughter's demands, be they parsimonious or extravagant.

For Lizzy and Jane, we had a nice double wedding and a lovely country meadow reception with fine pheasants, wine and a fiddler's trio calling the reels. A good time was had by all, country and city folk alike.

If you are in the mother-in-law position, I encourage you to accept your new daughter-in-law with open arms and, if possible, open heart as well. It will see you in good stead when the grandchildren arrive.

The in-law duties are to host the pre-wedding banquet for the wedding party and a few out- of-

town guests. Consult with your future daughter-in-law about the wedding guest list and abide by the parameters. If the second cousin twice removed must be struck off the list to keep the numbers manageable ——then struck she must be.

In some cases, the bride may be bereft of family and the groom's family provides the pre-wedding celebration as well as the wedding. If that be the case, treat the bride as a beloved daughter, and follow the same instructions for the mother of the bride.

There are pre- wedding events of which I have recently become painfully aware and do not approve. The odious tradition of a bachelor party for women, known as the bachelorette party, which sometimes takes place in far away places in establishments of questionable morals encourages most unladylike behavior. Such events should be avoided. The groom and his groomsmen also have their bachelor gathering in gambling establishments and clubs with bawdy

entertainment. I implore both sexes to desist in the participation of these vulgar events. It vexes me severely and puts me in the mind of what poor Lydia had to endure with that rogue, Wickham.

There are pre- wedding events, that are much more acceptable, such as the engagement party. Food and drink are provided, and a special toast is offered to the couple. Gifts are not required, but sometimes a small token is given. We provided a lovely gathering to announce Jane and Bingley's engagement, with Darcy's sister giving a tremendous piano concert. The surprise of the evening was Darcy himself, leaping to the stage afterwards to congratulate his sister and exuberantly announcing his engagement to Lizzy.

A gathering of the bride's female friends, aunts and cousins to celebrate her upcoming nuptials with gifts to help provide the beginning furnishing of her kitchen and linen cupboards is most acceptable. This type of event is usually organized by the bride's sisters, friends, or cousins.

♦♦♦

Thank Yous

"One ought to remember kindness received and forget those we have done." ... Seneca

Special handwritten notes of thanks must be delivered in response to gifts received, special visits, after dinner parties, and whenever one feels a formal appreciation of gratitude is needed. It is best to give thanks as close to the event as possible, but if one has forgotten or been delayed— — late is better than never!

Early Marriage

"Go now to your dwelling place to begin the days of your life together."… Apache wedding blessing

After having spoken the vows, do not assume dear ladies, that all will be well. To begin a life together is an exciting adventure, a romantic journey. But proceed with caution. What you do, what roles you assume in these early years are important.

Perhaps your husband has been under the wing of a doting mother who saw to his every care and concern. Perhaps he was accustomed to a household with several servants at his beck and call. Take care, my gentle women, not to take on a mantle of service. We ladies so easily see a need and hasten to fill it, wishing to start our married life doing things for our beloved.

My advice——write your husband a poem, massage his temples, but DO NOT pick up his

socks, clear his plate, manage his clothes or serve him food! The much- indulged male will leave his socks on the floor and curse when he cannot find things, expecting you to intercede. I caution you ladies: DO NOT and, I repeat, DO NOT intercede. With extraordinary strength of will and with every fiber of your being you must fight your natural inclination to step in and fix, mend, find, clean and take care of…

Remember, smile sweetly. If he asks where his such and such is, sweetly express concern that he cannot find it, commiserate with him, how terrible for him, how frustrated he must feel. Even if you clearly know where the item is, RESIST locating it for him! Trust me ladies: an accomplished suitor can quickly turn into a helpless husband, relying on his wife to shoulder all household burdens, and then blame her regarding the outcome.

If he complains that he has no clean socks, again, dear ladies, commiserate with him about his sockless situation. Resist the urge to wisk away the

pile of dirty socks growing daily by the bedside Sooner or later he will realize that he must get them to the laundress or, at least, put them where the weekly washing is done.

At meals, if it is just the two of you and there is no cook, consult with him about the menu. If he has skill in the kitchen, by all means encourage it. Collaborate on the meal. Make sure you are in the larder together, pulling things out for meal preparation. Make it fun!

If he clearly is all thumbs in the kitchen, tell him you need his company while preparing the meal. Make sure to ask him for assistance———setting the table, opening the wine, bringing a platter to the table, taking a heavy pot from the stove——— anything to involve him in the preparation of the meal. If you do this, you will never be relegated to kitchen duties, while he sits in the library waiting for the dinner bell.

After the meal if there is no household help, clear your plate and invite him to join you in the

kitchen. DO NOT PICK UP HIS PLATE! Now that you have him in the kitchen, ask him which he prefers———washing or drying. Or, if you have an area where your dishes are set aside for the morning servants, does he prefer to stack or to scrape? He may say "neither" and you must respond with humor and agree, saying you dislike this mundane chore too, but doing it with him makes it bearable. There now, no one can accuse of being a nag or a shrew.

These small things, socks, dishes, meals may seem petty. But keep in mind it is the everyday tasks that are essential to daily life. If you are shouldering the burden alone, tiny resentments will soon flare into full contempt.

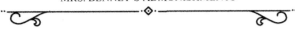

Marriage

"With all humility and gentleness, with patience, bearing with one another in love, eager to maintain the unity of the Spirit in the bond of peace." ... *Ephesians 4:2-3*

Looking at the larger picture, oh, what a joy the uniting of two souls is! To be in companionable partnership in heart, mind, body and soul. There is a sense of belonging, of recognition, a knowing, an understanding and treasuring of each other that says, "yes, this is the fit, the lock and the key." There will be differences, and sometimes the very differences in your natures may be what unites you. A cautious manner is encouraged by optimism, and an optimist is tempered by the cautious. The intellectual instructs the emotional, and the emotional brings feeling to the intellect. The introvert is drawn out by the extrovert, the extrovert is reined in from excess. As the taciturn

is charmed by the loquacious, the chatty one learns to listen. All is a balance.

Too often once we have found our match, we set about wishing for more similarity, losing sight of the valuable balance a difference of nature supplies to the union. Honor the gifts of self your partner brings to the union. Cherish the differences. As the Bible instructs————"Hold fast to one another."

Do not let other family members interfere with or disrupt your union. Guard your tongue. Do not gossip about your spouse's failings. Instead, seek to support any fragilities or deficiencies. How you think about your spouse influences how your spouse thinks about himself. Avoid telling him what to do, when to do it and how to do it. This may be the hardest thing to adhere to in a marriage. Merely reverse the situation: would you value a spouse who constantly instructed, cajoled or whined to have things done a certain way? Wouldn't it make you feel rebellious, resentful and

cause you to withdraw from the situation? The vow to honor means just that: to honor your spouse, give him space to accomplish what he must in his own way. Think about the fairy-tale prince, rescuing a damsel. What if the damsel instructed him to ride a certain way on a specific horse, use his sword a certain way to best cut through the bracket or climb up the tower using specific stepping stones. The prince would not only lose all enthusiasm for the damsel, but would carry out the task in a bored, resentful but dutiful way.

Intimacy

"Love is but a fire to be transmitted."... Gaston
Bachelard

Dear ladies, I will not belabor the delicate
nature of this subject. The most important thing in
creating intimacy is to remain open and vulnerable
with your husband. Allow him to know your fears,
your hopes and your wishes.

There are numerous manuals written as to
techniques and style. My one admonishment is to
SEEK YOUR OWN PLEAURE! In seeking it, he
will find this response exciting and pleasurable. Do
not expect your husband to always take the lead in
matters of love. He may have his foibles and
insecurities. A generous, loving wife can do much
to guide him in increasing skill to enhance her
pleasure.

Marriage can become routine. Variety within
the confines of wedded bliss is a must. Consider

the time of day. Night time does not always have to be the moment for sharing love. Where an act of love takes place may also enhance variety. The bedroom, though comfortable, can become boringly habitual. Consider a daring different location: a secret meadow, a carriage ride, a passionate embrace on the veranda while attending a Ball or an Assembly, even a surreptitious squeeze while out in public Something as simple as a seductive smile at a dinner party may be all the encouragement he needs. Flirt with your husband, rejoice in his manliness, compliment him on his physique, his intelligence. Most importantly, share a joke and laugh together, for that is the truest of intimacies.

To the newly married, I advise waiting five years to have children. I admonish you to create memories together as a wedded couple before the responsibilities of parenthood arrive. These memories will sustain you during difficulties. I advised Lydia to wait, and, luckily, she did. For as

you readers are most likely aware, she made a most odious match that could have resulted in an abandoned young mother. Even with staid Darcy and the affable Bingley, I cautioned both Elizabeth and Jane to have fun, go on adventures and travel. Bond with your husbands well before having children.

Income

"It is not inequality which is a real misfortune it is dependence."… Voltaire

Disparity in income between a husband and wife is always an issue. A wife's contribution to a marriage may come in the form of a dowry -- family name, title, land and her own income. A

husband may provide a home, land, his income and other holdings. After the marriage, I advise you to secure joint ownership of any land, country home, city dwelling and any stocks or bonds. Stress to your spouse, that in the event of one of you passing, joint ownership of all holdings ensures the care of the children and a secure future for all.

The terrible ordeal of an unusual entail, which caused us the loss of Longbourne, must be avoided. Mr. Bennet was not the actual owner of Longboune. He was the second cousin of Mr. Collins's mother; whose husband was the actual owner. When old Mr. Collins passed, Mr. Bennet, not being from the paternal line, was only allowed to live at Longbourne as a steward ensuring the farm's viability, managing its annuities until the only son of the owner became of age and married. Mr. Bennet could not stay on the property until his death. Only if the son had no interest in the estate, and Mr. Bennet had a son, to ensure the continuity

of property, could the entail have been redrawn favoring Mr. Bennet and his male heir. From this complexity of events the gentle reader might understand my reasonable anxiety for Mr. Collins to consider one of my girls as a suitable wife. But Lizzy rejected him, and Charlotte, being a woman of good sense, not to mention her family's large estate that abutted Longburne, saw an opportunity. She was delighted to learn she didn't have to wait for Mr. Bennet's death. Now with the birth of her son, the entailment is secure for Charlotte Lucas and Mr. Collins's male descendants.

I admonish you to be sure to check with your spouse about the status of all properties, investments, holdings, and possible inheritances that can give the advantage of ownership to your spouse.

As you have established the partnership allowing equal household management, so, too, must you establish an equal partnership in all

financial holdings. If you note your husband's furrowed brow when dealing with financial burdens, encourage discussion of his cares, fears, and plans. Be part of the planning process. This way you are not caught unawares and truly offer a partnership, instead of just being given a household allowance and told to economize.

During our marriage, Mr. Bennet and I tended to have one account. I contributed my artist commissions, and he, the sale of his manuscripts and essays. Unfortunately, Mr. Bennet was of a parsimonious nature, and I, if truth be told, was much more open-handed. Looking at the actual figures in the account and establishing goals together can circumvent many arguments.

Another possibility is to keep separate accounts. But, then I question, if both maintain financial independence, where then is the partnership? Perhaps the best course may be the major use of income as the focus of one account with the management for both to agree. Then the

use of smaller personal accounts can be for trivialities, which can be kept separate. I do caution you ladies, however, that small accounts can accrue large debts, especially if your husband has a weakness for cards and gambling.

Remaining open and above board in all things financial is best. Financial discussion must take place before any vows are spoken. Perhaps a meeting with a solicitor to start your married account together is best. If your betrothed refuses and wishes you not to have access and share ownership of all funds and properties——then, ladies, he is not the gentleman for you. DO NOT ACQUIESCE IN THIS! This issue is vital for an equal and balanced marriage.

In-Laws

"Old-fashioned ways which no longer apply to changed conditions are a snare in which the feet of women have always become readily entangled."… Jane Addams

Civility, respect and sometimes love are all parts of the equation of your relationship with your husband's parents. These people raised and cared for the son you love. Keep in mind, advice is not criticism. My mother-in-law used to offer her opinion on how things should be done, or furniture placed, and curtains hung starting with the phrase, "If I were you I would"…It set my teeth on edge until I realized——well she is she, and not me, and I could respond with gentle humor saying, "Well you are you, and not me, but thank you for the suggestion." She laughed and said, "You are going to do exactly as you please, aren't you?" I laughed with her, but added, "I'm glad you are there should I need you." You have

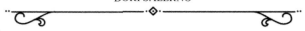

the ability to make your mother-in-law an ally or an enemy.

If you are the mother-in-law, I caution you to refrain from making comments about your daughter-in-law's culinary skills, house maintenance, child rearing, money management, relationship with your son or, indeed any aspect of the couple's life. Bear in mind, any criticism you have should be directed towards your progeny. If the house is unkept, diet unhealthy, children unruly, the husband bears the blame also. Blaming the daughter-in-law for your son's inadequacy as a house holder, parent and provider does nothing to improve the situation. A word of support for the wife: hands on assistance if she will accept it, and a gentle rebuke to your son to do his share will do much to earn her respect and esteem.

When you marry, you inherit a whole new set of relationships. I advise you to be civil and gracious to all. Do not get drawn into old family feuds. Sometimes, within this extended family you

may find a like- minded friend or ally. Much to my delight, I have two sisters- in- law, whom I esteem and respect. One is a highly skilled fellow artist, creating art that I find particularly soul moving; the other is my "comrade in arms." Knowing my secret abhorrence of entertaining, she rolls up her sleeves and makes the whole experience decidedly less painful.

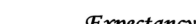

Expectancy

"Life is always a rich and steady time when you are waiting for something to happen or to hatch"... E.B. White

"Wishing you Joy." That is the phrase uttered by all to newly expectant mothers. You may recall, I erroneously wished Charlotte Lucas Collins joy on two separate occasions. The first occurred at the private breakfast meeting after our double wedding festivities. I misinterpreted Charlotte's flushed and anxious countenance as a possible sign of pregnancy, when, in fact, that sad day was the beginning of the loss of our beloved Longbourne. The second occasion happened at another private meeting with Charlotte at Rosings, when she again appeared blushing, and hesitant. Her reason, a caution about Darcy and Lizzy.

My point is, do wait until a lady has announced her joy, before wishing it. With fashions, and diets

changing so, fullness of petticoats, gowns, overcoats, and wraps, it is easy to misconstrue plumpness or a larger bosom as a sign of pregnancy and wish joy in error, causing much embarrassment.

Once joy is wished and, hopefully, you are joyful, bask in the attention of others. Enjoy your husband's solicitous concerns, your mother's affection, advice and ministrations, your friend's merriment and the appointing of the nursery.

When you have had enough and need rest, do not deny yourself: seek your own comfort, for only you know what is best. Follow the advice of the physician and apothecary as needed.

Each birth experience is unique; does one walk, stoop, breathe moan, cry during birth or become a mother by some other means All in the end comes to the same. Welcome to motherhood, a lifelong responsibility.

Motherhood

"A mother is she who can take the place of all others but whose place no one else can take."... Gaspard Mermillod

A mother no longer puts her needs first. Say goodbye to long, lovely baths, uninterrupted reading and sleep. You are now fully responsible for another human being's life. In the early years one is ever vigilant, getting up during the night for frequent checks, walking behind an unsteady toddler to prevent a cracked head, monitoring what goes into the body to provide nourishment, as well as what proceeds to successfully come out. Motherhood is not for the squeamish! Keeping a child healthy in mind, body and spirit is a daunting task. Every sniffle and cough must be attended to, every scrape and bruise cared for, every food monitored lest it be on the allergic list to be avoided. Stimulation must be provided for the

childrens' intellectual growth, through exposure to educational experiences, special lessons in music, art, or sport, whatever is suited to their talents. Social outings must also be planned to help cement friendships.

Motherhood, at times, can feel like the constant completion of tasks, and it is easy to become mired down in the details of it all. I admonish you at each stage of your child's life to take a moment, breathe, slow down and take the time to involve yourself in the special moments of their childhood. Look at the stars, blow bubbles, bake, read and paint together, snuggle, and share a laugh. Enjoy this special time together. The old adage is so true, "It goes by too fast."

As a mother to my girls, when they became of age, I admit I was obsessed with managing them, wanting them to have a settled life. All mothers want to see their children be successful in their endeavors, in marriage, as householders and as parents themselves. But I admonish you not to

make the mistakes I made. If you try to mold them into what you want and you believe you know best, as they grow into young adults, they may resent your interference and influence. Being a mother is forever; you must be there as best you can and do what is best for them. Sometimes not being there is best, lest they feel smothered; other times you must surround them with love, so they feel safe. Navigating the path between being stern and lenient while guiding them to adulthood is never easy. Letting go is the hardest part.

Care of the Infant

"They, who are so fresh from God, love us"....
Charles Dickens

There is no such thing as spoiling an infant. If the baby cries, she must be responded to immediately. An infant's cry is the way the child communicates. Failure to respond, thinking you can train a baby not to cry when in need, is monstrous. What you teach that dear little helpless one is that the world is a cruel place, and she is unloved. So many severe nannies insist on letting a child "cry it out." What happens is the child does finally stop from sheer exhaustion, her body fluids depleted by her tears. You will have created a fearful, insecure, repressed or angry little being.

If you have employed a nanny or baby nurse, I implore you ladies to hire those with the softest of hearts. I raised my own girls without nannies or governesses. I fed my children if they cried from

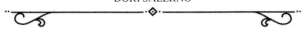
hunger and comforted them when they needed soothing. I am aware of the burden and tedium at times of mothering. Some part-time help can be beneficial to both parents. But mother and father should be the main source of care. Do not relegate your husband to secondary status in attending to the baby's needs. Many a fussy baby is much soothed by the strong shoulder, soft beard and low thrum of the male voice.

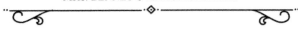

Children

"'Children need love, especially when they do not deserve it".... H.S. Hulbert

Bringing up five daughters, each with vastly different temperaments, was a challenge to be sure. The one thing I did learn through this exhausting experience is to honor their feelings. When a child is having a tantrum, it is caused by frustration, for the child cannot get what she wants. The best recourse is to help the child put into words what she wants—— "You want to stay in the meadow and are upset that we must leave. You wish you could stay longer." Stating the issues sometimes (not always) makes the child feel heard and understood. This technique usually helps to abate the tears, reducing them to sniffles as you continue to express your sadness that "We can't stay longer; Papa is waiting."——Notice, I did not give way and say we will stay longer——I held to

what must be done but honored her frustration, sadness, and anger.

This technique also works with older children. I have always regretted not noting Lydia's restlessness and need for attention. Had I discussed with her that it is natural for a young girl her age to be flattered, to have a crush, and had I warned her to come and speak to me before acting rashly, her unhappiness with Wickham might have been prevented.

But perhaps not. Lydia has a good heart, yet she has always been headstrong in her opinions. Love your children as best you can, support them, encourage them, but do not coddle, them keeping them dependent on you. They are separate human beings, not extensions of yourself.

This awareness of identity separation is most helpful from the years of fifteen onward. Once my girls were out of the schoolroom, and coming of age, that schism was necessary for survival. Though always their mother, I sometimes had to

hold on dearly to my sense of who I was, as I was often laughed at, condescended to, mocked, or outright ignored!

Grand Parents

"Hold on to my hand, Even if someday I'll be gone away from you."… Pueblo Prayer

Hey Ho! All the fun and none of the responsibility! Not quite— if you find yourself in the enviable position of being a grandparent, feel free to take delight in the sheer existence of that precious being. Yet understand there are responsibilities that must be undertaken. Grandparents are usually more indulgent and less rigorous about discipline than the child's parents.

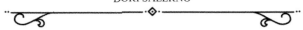

That is the natural order of things. However, as a grandparent, it is your duty to keep the child safe and to respect the parents' wishes regarding nutrition, routine, and bedtimes. Obviously when the child is under your care, there will be some leeway, but I admonish you not to flagrantly undermine parental guidelines or speak derogatively about their rules, or you may find yourself with limited access to the child.

Grandparents must offer a safe place where children can vent their frustrations and receive unconditional support and love. My girls did not have the luxury of my mother's grandmothering, as my mother passed away well before my children were born. However, they do have the wonderful opportunity of being loved, cared for and cherished by my husband's mother, a grand woman of heart and intellect. She encouraged them in their chosen path, soothed their insecurities and always demonstrated the greatest belief in their abilities. She is a woman of vision

and is convinced that my girls are destined for great things. My girls adore her, and she has been a great support to me as well.

If you are fortunate enough to have parents willing to assist you with your children, be sensitive to their needs. Don't assume that they are always available to step in and care for your children. They have lives of their own. It does not mean they don't love you or your children, if they travel and can't make a special occasion or are too frail to keep up with an energetic child.

Be open to their advice. They raised you and might know a thing or two about being a parent. Offering their opinion about the care of their grandchildren comes from love. Do not harbor any resentment about it. If they are not adhering exactly to your rules and restrictions and the child is in no danger, just be grateful they are in your children's lives. The more people who love your child, the better. Children can adapt. They understand grandparents' rules, and still respect

the parents' house rules.

Sometimes the reverse is true, and the grandparents expect more disciplined behavior than what is allowed at home. Experiencing different environments with different expectations helps to prepare a child for living in the world.

Mothers and Daughters

"Thou art thy mother's glass, and she in thee" ...
William Shakespeare

I have no sons, so I cannot comment on what that relationship is like. I have observed that mothers seem to be more indulgent with sons and expect more from daughters. Perhaps this behavior occurs because mothers see males as

alien, more fragile, the ego needing more support; whereas with daughters, the mother knows the inner strength and endurance of the female as they are the same sex. Blessed or cursed with the five I have, taken as a whole, they embody every aspect of a daughter—— dreamy, sarcastic, intelligent, passionate, shy, insecure and robust.

Wanting what is best for a daughter is one thing; doing what is best is another. Manipulation rarely works. I tried to manage the courtship of Jane and Bingley by refusing her the carriage. Unknowingly, I put her health at risk, in order for her to remain in Bingley's care, so he might fall in love with her. Fall in love he did, but he also abandoned her, being easily influenced by his friend. Of course, he eventually sought her hand, and that time spent with him certainly enhanced his feelings for her. But during the time of abandonment, how guilty I felt for all the pain Jane was suffering, feeling my actions had been the cause. I made the same mistake with Lizzy,

pushing her to consider Mr. Collins, and I had the audacity to be angry when she refused him! My point is: "Mother does not always know best." Pushing a daughter into a friendship you approve, a profession you admire, or a suitor you think would suit may accomplish the exact opposite. Though your intentions are well meant, your daughter may rebel, just to prove that she is different from you.

The hardest thing to do when you have a specific experience with something she is doing, is to hold your tongue. Your advice will be scorned and resented. However, if she seeks your opinion, do offer it guardedly, prefacing it with "Well, this worked for me, but it may not work for you." Then it becomes her choice to act on the advice with no blame.

Sometimes we underestimate our daughters and hover, concerned for their safety, while fearing that they may be attempting something beyond their ken. Let go and let them make the effort on

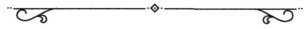

their own. They may surprise you. Offer your congratulations on their successes and comfort over their failures but take no responsibility for either. If you have provided them opportunities for a good education and a stable home filled with love, care and support, you have given them all they need.

Do not live through your daughter. Find fulfillment in your own life. The connection between a mother and daughter can at times be symbiotic and that symbiosis can be unhealthy. As your daughter ages, develops friendships, marries, and starts her own family, your input and influence should wane. During your daughter's period of confinement and early motherhood, however, be prepared for a resurgence of need. Reassure her about her abilities to mother, again offering advice only if asked and in the most temperate way.

Daughters, I admonish you to respect your mother. Get to know her as a person with her own history, life, hopes and dreams. Sometimes a friend

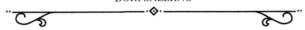

will say, "I enjoy talking with your mother." You may think, how can that be? Simple, your friend is able to experience her as a person with thoughts, ideas and accomplishments of her own not contingent upon your existence. Be grateful for all she has done. See her for who she is. You may find you have much in common, and when she is gone, you will miss her.

Siblings

"Blest Be The Ties That Bind Us"... John Fawcett

Siblings bound by blood, family, and shared memories must navigate the labyrinth of their relationships of kinship and rivalry, with patience, and hopefully, love. Watching my girls struggle with their differences, form sisterly alliances, break apart with harsh judgements and come together in understanding has deepened my respect for the sibling bond. Jane and Lizzy, my two eldest, have always been thick as thieves, and Kitty and Lydia, my two youngest were two peas in a pod. Poor Mary, being the exact middle, having little in common with either set, was a solitary soul but really was none the worse for it.

The problem arose between Lizzy and Lydia being "chalk and cheese," so unlike the other: Lizzy with her smart, sarcastic wit and Lydia with her exuberant, fun- loving nature. It is a wonder

that they could come to an understanding, but eventually they did, each slowly comprehending the difficulties in the other's life.

Being born into or being part of the same family does not guarantee immediate kinship. But childhood memories are shared: holidays at home, family rituals, family feuds, mutual understanding and sometimes humor at parental eccentricities, all weave the family web. As one ages, things mellow.

There are joys in siblinghood; laughter and love shared, care and concern. I was never close to my elder brother James, he, being much older and away in London. But when I was in need regarding Lydia's indiscretion, James Gardiner stepped in and with Mr. Darcy's assistance, provided the financial wherewithal needed to convince Wickham to "do the right thing." I will always be grateful to such a reliable brother and generous uncle

In observing the closeness of Jane and Lizzy and Lydia and Kitty, it is apparent how their

temperaments complement each other: kind and dreamy Jane, and witty sarcastic Lizzy, her tartness balancing her sister's sweetness, the very sweetness that prevents Lizzy from becoming bitter. Likewise, the same with Lydia and Kitty: sunny outgoing Lydia cheering up and encouraging Kitty and Kitty's shy natural reticence helping to damper Lydia's too high spirits. Each drawing upon the strengths of the other, a true balance of sisterhood.

Cherish your siblings if you can. Allow for their differences, quirks and eccentricities. Show compassion for their faults and forgive their transgressions. While Mary has no match within the family, no soul sister to share her thoughts, she is loved by all. Knowing she is loved at home, Mary has been able to excel scholastically away from home, while finding true fellowship among friends.

Friendship

"True friendship multiplies the good in life and divides its evils."... Gracian Baltasar

Friendships sustain us. Human connection to another is a basic need. A husband is a connection, family is a connection, but it is not the same as the delight of a friend. To share a laugh, a bit of gossip, big ideas or serious contemplation————someone to delight in your achievements and to share in your sorrows, someone to turn to for validation and truth. I urge you to seek that connection whenever possible. To be in the company of a good friend is truly balm for the soul.

Try to connect and find friends wherever you are. If in a group, or attending a lecture, there must be a like-minded soul you can connect with in some way. Reach out and make a friend.

I have never regretted any overture I have made, however shy or nervous I was to connect

with a potential friend. After a theatrical presentation I attended, I announced to the group that I sought someone to share the cost of a carriage, and lo and behold another woman took the offer. That carriage ride proved providential. Though we disagreed as to the import of the presentation, we found that our shared interest in the arts and the city bonded us. Feeling shy at first, I found the excuse of a special art exhibit to call upon her. Such delight did we share in each other's company and conversation over tea that we never did make it to the exhibit. Thirty-two years later, sharing the joys and sorrows of life, she is a special aunt to my children, indeed, she is even the one who encouraged me in my marriage, when I had doubts.

Friendships can be found in unexpected places. I remember meeting a special group of friends of my husband-to-be, expecting to find myself feeling alienated by this tight clique. Instead, I found a true soul sister, even though outwardly we

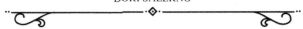

appeared opposite in our natures and pursuits. She encourages me in my wild schemes, and I am soothed by the calm report of her daily round.

Friendships must be maintained. Do not be too busy with your every day concerns to drop a line or two to inquire as to your friend's well-being. Be there for their triumphs as well as their failures. Lizzy and Charlotte were true friends. Lizzy delighted in Charlotte's mind and her calm and steady nature. I was concerned when Charlotte married Mr. Collins, fearing it would affect their bond, but Lizzy and Charlotte remained steadfast in their mutual admiration and devotion. Do not be so caught up in the affection of your beaux that you neglect your friends. Be sensitive to a friend's feelings of being left out, overlooked or forgotten. Make the effort to include them and find special time to reconnect. Most friends will understand if you are caught up in a heady romance and will be patient.

There are all kinds of friendships that occur

throughout one's life. Childhood friends like Lizzy and Charlotte, Mary's school friendship with Lady Amelia, and my own workplace friendship with Miss Elders, headmistress of the Abbey school, where I taught painting, come quickly to mind.

There are bonds often formed with others experiencing the same events in life; new mothers discussing infant care is a common one. Many a new mother is quite taken with her new friendships with young mothers like herself much to the dismay of her single or childless companions. I caution the young mother, though she delights in these new-found companions, sharing baby stories, child rearing techniques, nanny problems, to not cast aside previous associations. Make time to be with your friends, away from your child. Be sensitive and listen to their thoughts, concerns and what is important in their lives. Try not to prattle on about your little one's latest achievement. A sentence or two about "Johnny is walking now and gets into everything"

will suffice. If they want more information they will inquire.

If you are the single friend or have no children of your own, be patient with your friend's new-found love. For it is like finding a new love. Don't call on her when she is overwhelmed, expecting the same amount of attention. She does not have time for long conversations, when the baby starts to cry, and the toddler is pulling at her skirts. A day out together sans children would most likely be appreciated. She may be starving for adult conversation.

If you like children, offer her a day out perhaps for a beauty treatment, while you watch the children, and you may make new friend. You may delight in and find yourself bonding with her children. Two of my dear friends, from my time as a young single woman came to visit. They graciously "oohed and ahhed" over my children and offered me a night away with my husband. As they were both single gentlewomen with not much

experience with small children, I warned them about bath time. When one child was in the tub, the little one, even though she had been bathed, would try to climb in too; they must be on their guard. As expected, when we returned, they laughingly described how the little one was bathed and dressed in her sweet nightclothes, while the elder one was starting her bath. When my dear friend bent down to pour some lovely scent into the tub, and my other friend turned to ready the towels, the little one slipped right back into the tub like a mischievous porpoise, nightclothes and all.

My sweet companions tried to oversee the meals, bath time and bed time but seemed worn out by their one night's assignment, very glad of my return. They expressed amazement that I, alone, was managing the children and conceded that the two of them were not quite up to the task. They now understood that there is hardly ever any time to linger over one's morning tea, enjoy a bit of gossip from a surprise caller or even dash a note

off in response to a query. Each of these women friends have been unwavering in the support of my progeny in all their endeavors, but perhaps that long-ago glimpse into motherhood solidified their resolve to remain independent with no family responsibilities.

Once children have "flown the coop," your friendships will become more important to you. A friend will offer comfort and solace in hard times and laugh with you during good times

Making Calls

"I say it's perfectly heartless your eating muffins at all, under the circumstances."… Oscar Wilde

It is the height of rudeness to just show up at someone's door and expect to be received. Advance notice is a must. Seeing a main door unlatched for some air is not an invitation. Seeing a carriage in front of a home is not an invitation. An invitation to visit is either verbal or written in advance. Approaching a doorway on a whim is an extreme intrusion. I have a small work studio a few feet from my main abode. Many a person, perhaps bored and seeking something to do, has entered my side gate meandered along the path, and presented themselves at my threshold. I receive them with a smile through gritted teeth, return to the main house, and politely offer them a beverage. I listen to their tale of woe or some other pointless gossip, while inwardly seething at

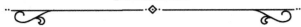

this invasion of my privacy.

To match their rudeness with rudeness is not an option. In truth, some family member in the main house may have just told them of my whereabouts and offered no limitations in regard to a visit. Communication of one's schedule is the best policy. Provide your family with the hours that you do not wish to be disturbed and encourage them to inform impromptu visitors of your unavailability.

If the visitor is at your door, you must be polite. A simple, "I am so sorry. I am working on a project right now and must keep my wits about me, might we schedule another time to get together?" should suffice. Invite them in but produce your calendar with pen in hand. Most will take the hint and schedule another time and leave promptly.

Proper hours of making calls should be honored. Early risers should be sensitive that not all are larks. Calls during mealtimes should never

be made, and evening calls should not be made past eight o'clock.

Gossip

"Happy the man who has never let slip a careless word, who has never felt the sting of remorse! Pleasant words win many friends, and an affable manner makes acquaintance easy"... Ecclesiastes The Book of Wisdom.

Sharing a bit of news, a little chat with a friend, so enjoyable. However, if the news maligns someone's character or makes sport of someone's misfortune, that dear ladies is just pure venomous gossip. Talk about ideas, philosophy, fashion, politics even, but resist sullying a person's

reputation or passing on news of a scandalous nature, whether true or not. Think before you speak. Will this information do damage? How much better to interrupt the gossipmonger with positive statements, finding something good to say instead. Having lived through such cruel chatter with my poor Lydia, I can attest to the "slings and arrows" suffered by our own family's heart. The snide comments by supposed friends, even as they partook of our hospitality at her post-wedding celebration, hit their mark. It was with much restraint, that I did not divert their vile gossip towards poor Georgianna, who suffered a similar fate from Wickham's debauchery. It would have accomplished nothing, ruined the reputation of Lydia and destroyed Georgianna.

Entertaining

"We'll have flesh for the holidays, fish for the fasting days. Moreover puddings and flapjacks and thou shalt be welcome"... William Shakespeare

I personally hate to entertain. The preparation: the writing of invitations, the shopping, the cooking, the house cleaning and cleaning of special china and crystal, the polishing of silver, the setting of the tables, and setting up the seating to everyone's advantage——all conspire to create a stressful event. Then there is the exhaustion from the tension of peacemaking and redirections of conversations to avoid potential arguments. Lest the reader forget, my true happiness lies in being solitary in a meadow, painting.

However entertaining is a social necessity. One must celebrate holidays with family and friends, and host dinner parties with special friends, neighbors and business associates. My favorite

thing to make for a gathering is——reservations——
—but no local inn has the capacity, availability or
varied menu that my soirees require.

Guests, I admonish you, PLEASE, PLEASE,
PLEASE DO NOT bring a dish to the party that
must be assembled or cooked in your hostess's
kitchen! If you feel you must bring something, a
bottle of wine or a pre-prepared dessert is
acceptable. A bouquet of flowers, however lovely,
is just a nuisance requiring the hostess to interrupt
her duties in the kitchen or her socializing with
guests to find a vase, fill it with water and place it
on display.

If you have special dietary needs, do make your
hostess aware but be reasonable. A severe allergy
should be mentioned. Your hostess may not
change the menu but can alert you to dangerous
foods. If you are adhering to a strict dietary regime
for weight loss or belief systems, it is best to keep
it to yourself and find something edible within the
menu. Vegetarians, wheat-free, or dairy-free

adherents can always find vegetables, salads, fruits, rice or potatoes without requiring a special dish be made.

As the hostess it is your responsibility to provide a warm environment, good food and drink, and greet guests enthusiastically, making them feel special. There are professional caterers and some inns do make food in quantities enough to satisfy your gathering but BEWARE! I availed myself of one recently, and the turkey dressing was so salty, the potatoes so pasty, that I spent much time in the kitchen "doctoring up" the dishes. Even the turkey had to be reseasoned. I might as well have made the whole thing from scratch, though it did save on preparation time.

Music is a lovely backdrop for social events but take care to keep the volume low so conversations can flourish. Sometimes a simple word guessing game can unite a group and make for much merriment.

Guests should never take it upon themselves to

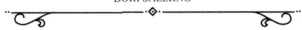
start clearing the table. If it is a formal dinner and staff are in attendance, there would be no need, and you would just embarrass yourself. If it is less formal and a table is laden with food, do not, in the guise of being helpful, start to clear off other guests' plates. The hostess, having just completed the preparations, for the buffet, the retrieving of last-minute guest requests and the seeing to everyone else's comfort, finally gets to sit and enjoy a glass of wine and her meal. Allow her the time to enjoy conversation at the table and finish her meal in a relaxed manner. Only when the hostess gives the signal that the meal is over and dessert may commence, may one assist in clearing if there is no staff. Please follow the hostess's wishes. If you are instructed to leave the plates in the kitchen and return to the dining room for coffee, tea, cognac and dessert, do so. Do not go to the sink to start scraping and rinsing. This is not your home.

After the repast, thank your host and hostess

for their hospitality. Leave taking should not occur abruptly; plan to linger at least 20 minutes after dessert. Keep in mind the energy the host and hostess have expended for the event. Staying past 90 minutes after dessert, unless prevailed upon specially to remain, is excessive.

A thank you note for the event should be sent within the week.

Entertaining Outside The Home

"Meat is much but manners more"… Proverb

Oh, it is with such delight to make my favorite thing——— Reservations! To sit with a like-minded friend or couple, enjoy a meal, conversation and laughter, what a delight! If you have proffered the invitation, then you are the host and must bear the cost. If your guests offer to pay, you must refuse. If you are the invitee, it is good manners to offer to pay or at least split the cost. The correct etiquette is for the host to refuse to accept the offer, but don't show your surprise if it is accepted. Pay with good grace and next time pre-set the conditions of payment. For couples who know each other well and share a similar financial status, a split is most amicable.

I recall years ago, that I was assiduously persuaded to invite my mother-in-law, a formidable woman of renown, to lunch, then to

speak at a special event. My acquaintance prevailed upon the connection of our daughters' friendship and beseeched me to make the lunch and speech happen. My mother-in-law acquiesced and consented to the luncheon as well as the speech. At the end of our lunch when proffered the bill, my acquaintance started to calculate what each of us owed. I remember being appalled, and my mother-in-law, as the guest speaker for this woman's organization, was justifiably affronted. I quickly offered to pay the bill.

Assistance

"Appreciation is a wonderful thing: It makes what is excellent in others belong to us as well."... Voltaire

All of us require help. Whether it be in the home, in the garden, with our hair, with our clothes, or with our deliveries. How we deal with and show gratitude for that help is important. Do not be miserly in your remuneration for services provided. Be mindful of the monetary difficulties faced by your helpers. Delays in payment can affect them quite severely.

For long-term faithful service in your home or property, a generous bonus at holiday time is required. Smaller gifts of gratitude should be given to your postman My dear postman this holiday sent a heartfelt note of thanks for my small token, as he stated he is so often overlooked by others. Those who collect the refuse from your home also should not be forgotten.

Those who provide personal services, hairdressers, seamstresses, medical attendants should all receive a note of thanks and some token, be it monetary or some gift they would like of home baked goods or special delicacies.

Remembering those who help us in our daily round, by showing gratitude for their assistance with words and deeds, will be repaid to you tenfold when you are in need of their assistance. Showing that you are not reluctant to roll up your sleeves and join in is most appreciated, for it takes many hands to run a home. Though your housekeeper may say it is not necessary to strip the beds and bring the linens to the laundry, she is secretly grateful that you are helping her.

Accomplishments

"Not what I have but what I do in my kingdom."… Thomas Carlyle

Enjoy the satisfaction of completing a task, learning something new, or reaching a goal. Do not downplay your achievement, compare it to others or fret it is not good enough, using some invisible unattainable standard measured by your insecurities. Too often I hear women make self-deprecating remarks about their successes and extol their failures. Perhaps they hold the false belief that this is the appropriate manner to demonstrate modesty for their ability. Think about this. What if a dear friend had finished a beautiful piece of embroidery, and as you compliment her on her fine handiwork, she then proceeds to tell you of all her attempts with tangled threads, missed stiches and bloodied cloth from pin pricks. Would you not remember more her tales of woe

than her success? Better for her to accept the compliment graciously with a "Thank you, it is a most intricate pattern." Do not be over-modest in your successes. Accept the praise given for your well-earned achievements without a disclaimer.

If an accomplishment is not rewarded, either monetarily or with special notice, does that make the journey to the goal and the goal itself worthless? Think of the great artists, musicians, philosophers and scientists overlooked, derided, and dismissed, never knowing acclaim or praise, some dying in poverty. Following your passion, your ideals and reaching your goals, whatever they may be, will give you the inner satisfaction of knowing you continued to persevere through failure, despair and even success. Sometimes the complacency of success can make one lazy, causing one to stop striving, learning or improving.

Accomplishments and achievements do not have to be great triumphs. They can include the

simple successes in your daily round of housekeeping, raising a child, gardening, or cooking a meal. I was most successful in raising my five daughters, handling their marriage prospects to the best of my ability, sometimes with success sometimes not. My artistic endeavors also brought me much satisfaction. Though my portraits were a success, I continued to paint in new ways that were challenging and personally rewarding. I exhort you to seek your passion, your own sense of success in whatever endeavor suits you.

Betrayals

"Most smiling smooth detested parasites"...
Shakespeare

Making a friend, a true friend, is not easy. Take your time in developing a friendship. Allow it to unfold naturally. Be in no hurry to divulge your darkest secrets, desires or wishes lest they be tossed about in gossip or mockery. Be wary of friends who are loyal only if it suits them. They are many who are fine friends during the good times, enjoying the comforts of your home and hearth and your connections in society or business. When there are difficulties, however, they are nowhere to be found. If a friend responds to your needs only at their convenience, then she is not a true friend. Repeating your confidences to others, making snide remarks at your expense under the guise of humor, are all forms of betrayal. Do not suffer these slights in silence. Challenge her remarks

privately. She may deny that it was her intent to demean you and defend her remarks as harmless, but if you feel harmed ——Do not waver! If she is a true friend, she will make a sincere effort to apologize, and seek to be in your good graces again. A betrayer will use the private conversation as a public quarrel, asking mutual friends to take sides in the matter. Your only recourse is immediate distance from the betrayer and a refusal to discuss it with others. If you resist the urge to respond to any public discourse about the disagreement, it will soon fade, and your betrayer will be frustrated in her efforts to engage you in further argument. Others will find her constant complaint a bore and she will be excluded from your circle.

Infidelity

" To have and to hold from this day forward forsaking all others."… Traditional church vows

A vow is vow is a vow is a vow. Careful when you make it, and woe to those who break it. Forsaking all others. What does that vow mean? It means loyalty to each other, over anyone else——parents, siblings, in laws, friends, children. Yes, even the children, for if mother and father are not faithful in their love for each other, the foundation upon which the family was created will disintegrate. What causes a spouse to stray? A shrewish wife? An indifferent husband? Perhaps indifference makes a shrew. Like the old conundrum of the chicken or the egg. It doesn't matter the cause. It all starts with failing to be faithful in the love for each other.

If you have suffered an infidelity, how to deal with it is the question. Rage, hurt, humiliation are

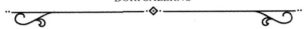
all normal responses. I caution you, however, that while in the throes of these very justifiable emotions, do not make any decisions.

Keeping a cool head will be of most benefit. Once an infidelity is discovered, it may be best to avoid confrontation or acknowledgement. The first step, before any accusations are spoken is to assess one's financial position. Gaining knowledge of all accounts and financial status is essential. Keep your counsel and investigate quietly all bank and stock holdings. Gather as much information as you can. This will help you make an informed decision if one decides to divorce.

Once there has been an admission of guilt, the response can go either one of two ways: sincere remorse or blatant disregard. Even if there is remorse, the marriage may be irreparable. There may be many protestations that it was just one happenstance. But one happenstance or a thousand makes no difference. The heart is broken just the same, the vow to be faithful in love to each

other has been violated. Only you can decide if you are able to continue together. If there are children involved, it makes it much more difficult.

If there are no protestations of love and remorse, only demands for freedom, grant it quickly. Do not hold on to hopes of his coming to his senses, realizing you are the better choice, remaining for the sake of the children, and so on. You are worth more than having a resentful husband, staying out of a sense of duty. It will only make you and your children miserable.

I do, however, in the case of a remorseful spouse or insensitive lout, have a suggestion I hope you will follow. Now is the time to get away. Your children should be safe with their father for a month and a fortnight or two. You must immediately go away, somewhere where you have always wanted to go to refresh your spirit. Travel can be so invigorating, a change of scenery, a relief of family duties, a time to indulge yourself.

This move accomplishes two things for the

husband who is bereft: he will go mad with missing you, worrying about you; and now that he is alone, he must cope with all family duties and children on his own. You needn't take others into your confidence, merely put it out to your mother or sister that you need some time away, are feeling a bit taken for granted, and wish to have your spouse appreciate all you do. You request, that if he seeks help from them, they should find themselves otherwise occupied. Make sure to cancel any usual household help before you leave and remove any ways of contacting them. Usually husbands do not have numbers of household help or childcare workers amongst their papers.

For the husband who demands his freedom, this will put a damper on any retreat to a love nest. Either his paramour will come into the home and assume all the family duties which she may find a bit wearing. Better still, make the main family home unavailable so all must move in with her for a short period of time. Having disgruntled children

about, whether moody teenagers or tantruming toddlers, strains any relationship. The romantic coupling rapidly changes into a daily grind of child care, school runs and dinners at home.

While you are away, your spouse should be able to contact you in the case of a real emergency, but only respond to real emergencies, someone in hospital, or a severe accident. Anything needing mending or fixing or sorting is not a reason for you to return. You can and should contact your children, encouraging them to carry on with their schedules and routines. Instruct them to rely on their father as needed and that you will return soon with some lovely gifts for them. If the children are unaware of the marital issue, a white lie that you must tend to a sick friend might suffice. If they are aware, just tell them often that you love them very much, will return, but are taking some needed time away. This time alone in new surroundings gives you the respite to either mend your broken heart and forgive, or gather the strength needed to plan

for a future that does not include your spouse.

None of this is easy, and I do not wish to make light of the hurt and humiliation. I merely wish to give you a sense of control. If you do decide that you can muddle along together, realize that the purity of the vow has been permanently stained. I caution you to keep a small part of yourself secreted away, untouchable and, protected.

If you find that you are that other woman, that paramour, I hope you ken that someone willing to break a vow may also not honor one with you.

Unsuitable Marriages

"Marry in haste repent at leisure."… William Congrave

There are times when it becomes clear that a marriage must end. Affairs, abuse and addiction are the culprits. Affairs break the vow of faithful love; abuse breaks the vow of honoring spouse and children; addiction breaks the vow of cherishing no other by cherishing a substance or a behavior above all else.

My dear Lydia, married so young, unable to see through the charms of her "Wickie" suffered all of the above. If you find yourself in a similar situation, I implore you to call upon your inner strength and leave. Safety for yourself and your children is the first priority. If you have a friend, sister, or cousin who may have fallen into these circumstances, reach out to her, bring her to safety, bolster her courage, lend her your strength.

It is my conceit that those reading these Gentlewomen Admonishments would never find themselves in such predicaments. However, a lapse in judgement, caused by romantic hopes can happen to anyone.

In truth, I was always concerned about Lizzy in her marriage to the dark, brooding, opinionated Mr. Darcy. Though he is a gentleman and appeared to dote on her early in their marriage, she was a bit cowed by entertaining the "Great and the Good" of society. His expectations of her behavior as a hostess were a bit stifling. I counselled her to be true to herself, sharpen her caustic wit and poke some fun at the pompous.

Beauty

"I never saw a woman so altered"... Oscar Wilde
"Beauty is as beauty does"... Chaucer

One often hears she was a great beauty or had a striking countenance. These comments describe the outward appearance, not the inner being. So much energy is put into enhancing personal appearance, often at the expense of developing character. I am not averse to one looking one's best, but the obsessive attention lavished upon the effort to deny the natural progression of age has become ludicrous.

I have seen women with bee-stung lips the size of platypuses and cheeks plumper than a nut-storing squirrel. I have seen eyes drawn upward into an unnatural slant with skin so tight that I feared any natural smile of delight would cause a split over the already enhanced cheekbone.

There is beauty in nature, beauty in the garden,

beauty in the design of a home and its furnishings Anything over-worked to an unnatural state, be it a face, figure, garden, or home loses all sense of any proportional aesthetic pleasure.

I have a friend who could not abide disfigurement of any kind. If she saw a person on the street with a limp or some form of disfigurement, she was violently repulsed by it and immediately sought distance from the person offending her sensibilities. When on my daily rounds tending to the sick or mentally frail, she could not understand how one could do so. She was not a bad person; she was a good wife, devoted mother and a dear friend, but illness or deformity frightened her. I offered her a simple technique. Gaze into the eyes of every person and connect soul to soul. If you quietly share this gaze, you will see the real person not the outer appearance. I am happy to report that my dear friend was able to be of service to others. She acquired a large, overly affectionate rambunctious

dog. She needed to focus his energy and decided to visit those in need with her dog. Through her animal's affection for all, she was able to overcome her aversion to imperfection and see the beauty in others.

Be you plain or comely, let kindness, compassion, and sincerity be your guideposts. A truly beautiful person is one who behaves beautifully towards others.

Charity

*"No one is useless in this world who lightens the
burden of it for anyone else."… Charles Dickens*

Seeing a need and responding. If food,
clothing, or alms is required, filling that need is
essential. However, the manner in which one
provides assistance is crucial. When I resided at
Longbourne, we made frequent visits to the less
fortunate, bringing along a basket of goods, a little
calf's foot jelly, produce from the farm, a knitted
shawl or two and some apothecary remedies.

Sometimes my girls would accompany me. Jane
was too distracted and dreamy to be of much help.
Lizzy was too embarrassed and judgmental. Kitty
was too shy to offer any comfort, and Mary was
too bookish and remote. I was most grateful for
my dear Lydia's presence. She had the ability to put
those impoverished households at ease with her
sunny nature. She was always ready to lend a hand.

She would reach out for the squalling baby, as I tended the mother. She was not averse to giving a dirty tyke a quick wash, or pick up a broom if needed, while I set a meal.

I see many society ladies swanning about, chairing committees to gain social standing, showing off their expensive gowns at gala charity events, without a clue or a care about the possible recipients. I say "possible recipients." Too often I have purchased tickets, persuaded Mr. Bennet to attend, only to find that the donations have been used to cover the cost of the hall, the food and the entertainment, leaving very little to the actual charity. Everyone had a wonderful time; photos were published in the social registry and society pages at the expense of those still in need.

Due diligence must be used to evaluate any cause that you support. Charitable funds used mainly for administration costs and salaries of those purporting to work for the charities must be avoided. A much better solution is to get involved

with the actual people in need, bringing food, blankets, and comfort. See the person in need as your equal, human-to-human contact. It will enrich your soul. When you help others, the ones helped also help you. If there is acknowledgement of this dynamic, dignity is preserved. It is never a "We versus them; it is an us."

Identity, The Authentic Self

"To Thine own self be true."..., William Shakespeare

What defines us? Our roles—— mother, daughter, wife, sister, friend? No! All the roles we play do not really define us; it is how we embody those roles, drawing upon our authentic self to fulfill them, that defines us.

There is an inner essence, a deep awareness of who we are, a feeling, a recognition, a sense of clarity. How does it manifest itself to us? We often glimpse our authentic self by our response to a piece of art, a passage in a book, a song lyric, or a moment in nature. Our soul, our inner self, acknowledges the recognition with a gasp of delight, a shiver of excitement or, perhaps a sigh of contentment.

Suppressing the authentic self can actually be damaging to one's health. I have witnessed many a

lady suffering severe migraines trying to conform to her husband's controlling behavior. I have also seen a mother, trying to parent difficult children, losing herself in the process. Too often a woman is the constant caretaker of others, busy running their errands, managing their issues, seeing to their needs at the expense of her own.

Ignoring the authentic self manifests in many ways: headaches, fatigue, digestion issues, dietary imbalance———either overindulgence or loss of appetite———extreme irritability, excessive use of alcohol or stimulants or any chemical means to dampen one's true feelings. I have watched many a lady fortify herself against anxiety with frequent inhalations of smelling salts, wrapped in her hankie. Many others liquify their anger with "medicinal" brandies and cognacs.

How does one find one's true authentic self again? Due to years of denial, it may be difficult to unearth. Start in small ways. As I write this, I realize the bouquet I just placed on my table

honors my authentic self in a simple and gratifying way. I have before me a simple blue ceramic vase of sunflowers and blooming rosemary. I plucked the rosemary from my garden, purchased a small bouquet of sunflowers from a vendor, and placed them in a vase. Simple things one would think, but, as I gaze at them, I remembered all the steps that led up to this small expression of my authentic self.

Several years ago, I attended an afternoon fund raising event that my husband refused to attend. I felt it was important to support the cause, and, much to my husband's surprise, decided to go alone. At the event many things were up for auction, which I could not afford but at the table were lovely centerpieces. Aha! There was the blue vase! I persuaded the hostess of the event to allow me to purchase the vase. It was a small pittance compared to the auctioned items. Coming home with my treasure, I heard my husband grumble at the purchase, thinking it had been part of the auction. I reassured him that the sum was small,

and I paid for it with the cash I had on hand.

The sprigs of rosemary had come from the wild rosemary bushes that I had prevented the gardener from removing. He insisted on pruning them back a bit, but that was all I would allow. Their scent and delicate blue flowers had delighted me. The sunflowers displayed on a street cart caught my eye. I walked past the vendor, but then retraced my steps and bought them on a whim.

Responding to something that calls to your soul is the way back to discovering your authentic self. Honor the whim, the idea, the event, which is a signal, a signpost pointing to your inner essence. If you find yourself feeling stubborn about something, like me with the rosemary bush, that stubbornness is a reaction to the self, needing to be recognized.

Reward yourself. It does not have to be monetary. If you cook for your family and they despise a food you like, make a portion of it for yourself. As you enjoy it, your family may respond

with "ewws and yucks," but may be intrigued by your resolute enjoyment and may even try it themselves! If your taste in music, poetry, or drama differs from your husband, don't be cowed by his contempt. Attend the concert, reading or play yourself. Your spirit will be refreshed.

Another essential tool to unearth the true self is to carve out time and space that is yours alone. Decorate and energize your area with things that touch you in some way. These may include a wall color, photo, quote, special book, piece of art, wall hanging, music, letters or cards, whatever keepsakes that are of value to you, a shrine to the self. Or if there is no space in your home, discover a quiet space on a walk, near a park, or a tea shop. Gaze about to see what brings you joy and contentment, bring a favorite book, eat a special lunch.

The important thing is to create the time and space to be alone without the chattering demands of others. I am aware that this might seem a

daunting task with conflicting family needs, social requirements and the stuff of daily life. There is one panacea that works: simply use the words "I can't." It is not a direct no. Some will respond, "Well, why not?" Be gracious, smile and reply, "I just can't." It is surprisingly effective. Your husband calls about dinner. You reply, a simple "I'm sorry, I just can't make it tonight" He will show up with a meal for the family and most likely respond with "I hope you are feeling better." You didn't say you were sick; you just said you couldn't do it. The same applies for any demand on your time by others. If asked to do an errand, handle an appointment or provide some assistance on a committee, you will discover people will find other ways to get their needs met. Another will be called to provide the ride, pick up the package, or serve in the group. Replying with "I can't" makes others think you are otherwise engaged. You are not lying, you are otherwise engaged, connecting with your authentic self.

This break from demands will help you connect with your authentic self. You can resume whatever role is required at the moment, be it wife, mother, daughter, or friend, now operating from the center of your authentic self. You will be happier in whatever role you are fulfilling, and others will be happier in your presence.

Connecting with your authentic self takes practice. You will know when you are disconnected. If you feel put upon to do some service and are not doing it joyfully, or you are missing an event that you wanted to attend or attending an event you wish you hadn't, the disgruntlement reflects a sense of disconnection. Feeling extremely out of sorts with your family is also a sign. We all say, "yes" to things we wish we hadn't.

Taking the time to find something that delights one's soul will do much to help in coping with the pressures of life. Keeping a journal of your thoughts, impressions and reactions is also an

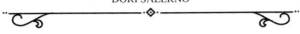

excellent way to unearth your true self.

The inner journey to your authentic self is lifelong.

Enjoy it!

No more admonishments, no more cautions or gentle scoldings. May these merely serve as motherly reminders from one who has erred many times.

Acknowledgements

Special thanks to Katherine Elswick for her encouragement, Deborah Donovan for her guidance, Carol Pratt for her editorial skill and Kevin Kornburger for his technical expertise.

Author Bio

 Dori Salerno is also the author of the novel, **_Mrs. Bennet's Sentiments,_** which received the People Magazine's top new fiction pick in November 2016. She has enjoyed creating the new companion piece, **_Mrs. Bennet's Admonishments._**

Under her theatre name, Dori Salois has been the Artistic Director of Vantage Theatre since 1994 and is now the Executive Artistic Director. She has produced with San Diego Repertory and La Jolla Playhouse, presenting Anna Deavere Smith's New York production of _Let Me Down Easy_ in association with Arena Stage's national tour. As a director and producer, Ms. Salois has brought over 37 plays to fruition.

She most recently produced Jesse Kornbluth's play, _The Color Of Light_ about Matisse's life, as a world premiere in San Diego in January 2018. This play went on to receive a New York production in April of 2019.

Ms. Salois has written and directed for television, *So This is Washington* and *West of Hedon*. She has also written for the theatre, co-authoring the plays *The Importance of Being Earnest the Musical!*, and *The Holy Man*, an adaptation of Susan Trotts novels; and *Macgregor*.

As an actor, Ms. Salois has performed in professional theatres, as well as film and television in New York, Los Angeles, Massachusetts, Washington D.C., and San Diego. Ms. Salois has received her Baccalaureate from Lowell University and her Masters from Georgetown University. She resides in La Jolla with her husband, is the mother of two grown daughters and writes fiction under her married name, Salerno.

Printed in Great Britain
by Amazon